Adventures
of The
STEM Brothers

Science - Technology - Engineering - Mathematics

Written by: Rhea Miles

Illustrations by: Annamarie Lewis & Kyra Miles

TAYLOR MADE PUBLISHING

ISBN 978-1-7330992-0-2

Cover by Annamarie Lewis & Kyra Miles
Interior Illustrations by Annamarie Lewis

Published by Taylor Made Publishing
www.taylormadenc.com

This book is dedicated to my father.

~

"I want to be a mathematician." –Johnny
"I want to be an aerospace engineer." –Thurman
"I want to be a computer software engineer." –Vernon

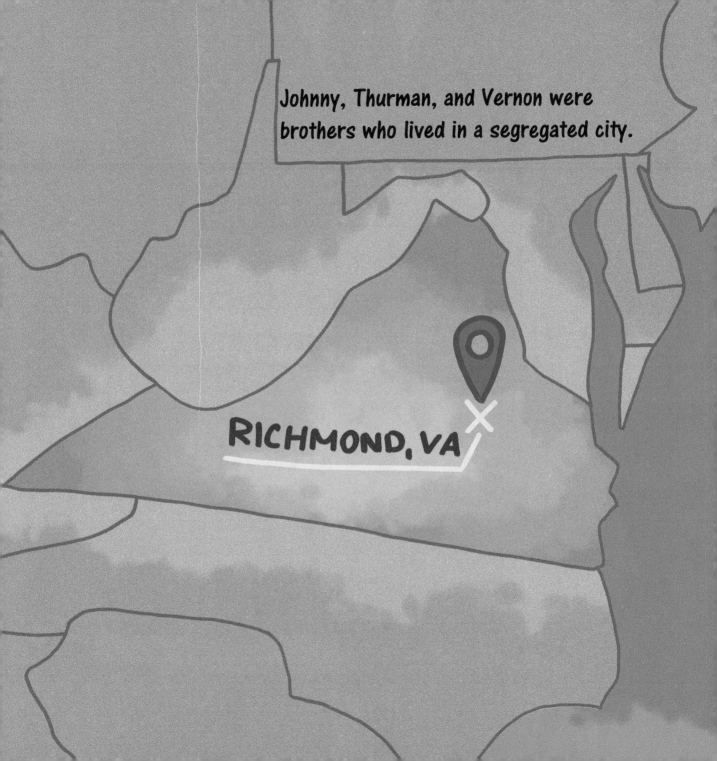

In their school, books were old and outdated; oh, what a pity.

LITERATURE 1942

SCIENCE

MATHEMATICS

They shared a love for mathematics, science, and sports.

PLAYING

STUDYING

THURMAN

JOHNNY

VERNON

All three earned college diplomas in STEM, of course.

Johnny worked at a phone company and used his mathematics degree.

"This is where phones will be used by consumers," he shouted with glee.

Some sabotaged Johnny's work and said, "he's overrated."

"Be first class in everything you do."

And Johnny continued to do his best and he married a lady mathematician.

They had a son and two daughters: a school administrator, professor of science and the other a physician.

Johnny 's brother, Thurman, attended college and he felt isolated.

The owner of a restaurant did not want Thurman there, so he reluctantly vacated.

A Few Moments Later...

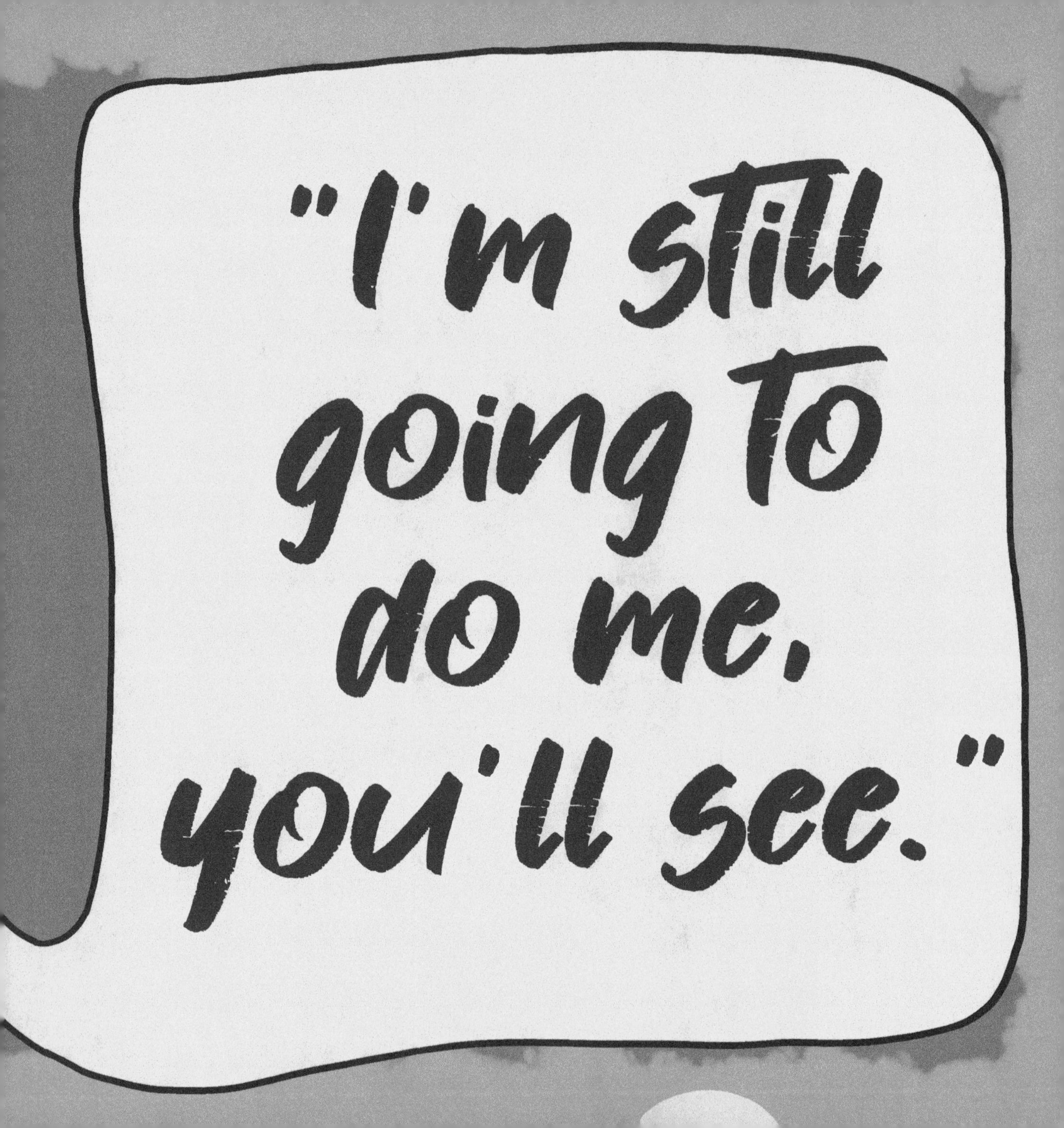
"I'm still going to do me. you'll see."

He graduated and served in the military, where he was decorated.

City Man Honored For Vietnam Service

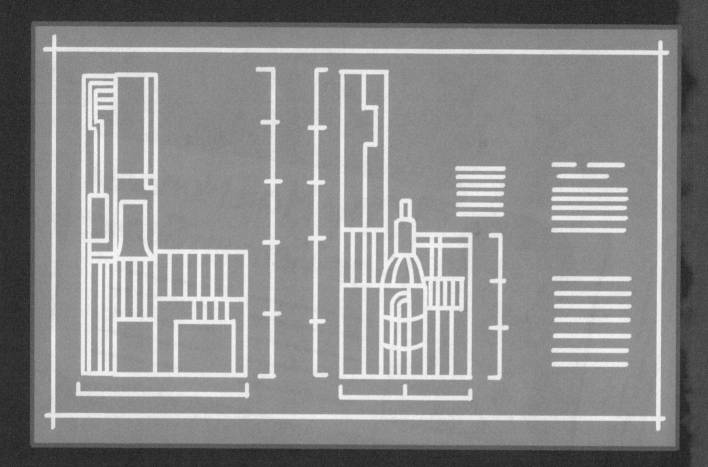

He was an aerospace engineer, and known
for innovative designs he created.

Thurman got married and had a son and a daughter;
she earned a medical degree and was highly rated.

Johnny and Thurman's brother, Vernon, did not want to be an aerospace engineer or work with phones.

Vernon became a software engineer who programmed computers to calculate unknowns.

Co-workers were credited for his ideas and not their own.
My
~~Vernon's~~
Plan!
You did this? Great Job!

People were not nice to him at his work...
HE SHOULD JUST QUIT!
LET'S KEEP STEALING HIS WORK! HAHA!
"I'm going to do me, you'll see."

So, Vernon found employment elsewhere and had a great year.

With perseverance and a great working environment, he earned awards and was promoted with cheers.

He got married, had three daughters, and one became a mechanical engineer.

...work hard and have fun with those who supported their dreams, too.

PROMOTION TO SR. PROGRAMMER

City Man Honored For Vietnam Service

What will you set your STEM mind to do?

GEOGRAPHER • BIOMEDICAL ENGINEER • MATERIALS SCIENTIST • COMPUTER SYSTEMS ADMINISTRATOR • ENVIRONMENTAL ENGINEER • STATISTICIAN • COMPUTER SUPPORT SPECIALIST • FORENSIC SCIENCE TECHNICIAN • WEB DEVELOPER • ACCOUNTANT • COMPUTER SYSTEMS ANALYST • GEOSCIENTIST • POSTSECONDARTY ENGINEERING TEACHER • COMPUTER NETWORK ARCHITECT • CARTOGRAPHER • PSYCHOLOGIST • EPIDEMIOLOGIST/MEDICAL SCIENTIST • FINANCIAL ANALYST • CIVIL ENGINEER • MECHANICAL ENGINEER • DATABASE ADMINISTRATOR BIOCHEMIST • COMPUTER & INFORMATION RESEARCH SCIENTIST • PETROLEUM ENGINEER • INFORMATION TECHNOLOGY MANAGER • INFORMATION SECURITY ANALYST

SOFTWARE ENGINEER • MATHEMATICIAN • AEROSPACE ENGINEER

Activities

Ask your parent or family member if they have a STEM job.

Read the list of STEM jobs in the back of the book. Research a STEM job you would like to do.

Has anyone ever stopped you from doing what you want to do?

GLOSSARY

Aerospace Engineer: Someone who works with and makes planes and spaceships.

Biomedicine: A type of medicine that works on a very specific part of your body.

Chemist: A person who is trained to do science tests in chemistry.

Computer Software Engineer: Someone who uses math, science, and design to make computers work.

Mathematician: Someone who works with numbers and math to solve problems.

Mechanical Engineer: Someone who designs, builds, and tests machines.

Physician: A doctor.

Science Educator: Someone who goes to school to teach science.

Statistician: A person who puts together numbers, pictures, and information to solve problems.

STEM: Science Technology Engineering Mathematics

ABOUT THE AUTHOR

Rhea Miles is an associate professor in science education at East Carolina University in the department of Mathematics, Science and Instructional Technology. Her publications have focused on under-served and underrepresented groups in STEM living in the United States. She is married to Gera Miles Jr. who also works at East Carolina University as a visiting lecturer. Together they have two children Kyra and Bishop (BJ). Rhea Miles was the first African-American female to earn a PhD at University of Virginia in science education and the first African-American female to earn tenure as an associate professor in science education at East Carolina University.

CPSIA information can be obtained
at www.ICGtesting.com
Printed in the USA
LVHW022358020919
629674LV00010B/982/P

9 781733 099202